KT-210-243

This igloo book belongs to:

....

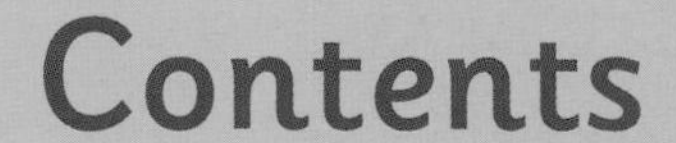

Contents

igloobooks

Published in 2014
by Igloo Books Ltd
Cottage Farm
Sywell
NN6 0BJ
www.igloobooks.com

FIR003 0514
4 6 8 10 9 7 5 3
ISBN: 978-1-78197-327-1

Printed and manufactured in China
Written by Xanna Chown
Illustrated by Bella Bee

Bedtime Stories for Girls

igloobooks

Bonny's Bedtime

It was Bonny's bedtime, but she didn't want to go to sleep. "I feel wide awake," she said to her dad. So, Bonny's dad tucked her up in bed with her cuddly, brown teddy, but Bonny still didn't feel sleepy. "What if I am awake all night?" she asked.

Dad smiled. “Don’t worry,” he replied. “I’ll tell you a special bedtime story.” Bonny nodded, so he began. “Once upon a time, there was a girl called Bonny,” he said. “She lived in a magical land where all the animals could talk.

One day, Bonny got lost in the woods. It was nearly bedtime, so she asked Owl if she could sleep in his nest for the night. Owl said yes, but when Bonny climbed into his nest, she found it was a bit too small and prickly for her to get comfy.

Bonny asked Fox if she could share her den for a night. Fox said yes and Bonny crawled in, but it was very squashed in the den and Bonny didn't like it at all. She climbed out and searched the wood to find somewhere else to sleep.

Bonny asked Deer where she slept and Deer showed her the clump of bushes she liked best. Bonny tried to curl up like Deer, but she soon felt very cold. Bonny began to miss her warm, comfy bed. "I want to go home," she said and she felt very sad.

Suddenly, a trail of glowing fireflies flitted past. They stopped to ask what was wrong. When Bonny told them, their little lights flickered in excitement. “Don’t worry,” they said. “We can show you the way home. Then, you won’t be lost any more!”

Bonny followed the fireflies along the path. They went past Deer, Fox and Owl on the way home. When Bonny arrived, she gave her dad a huge hug! He tucked her into bed, where she went to sleep right away and that is the end of the story."

"That was a lovely story," said Bonny. "Was it about me?" she asked, giving a big yawn. Before Dad could answer, Bonny had closed her eyes and was fast asleep. "Goodnight Bonny," he said, gently. "Sleep tight and dream of all your forest friends."

Wildlife Walk

Lisa had come to stay with her grandma and they were reading a book about jungle animals. There were photographs of roaring lions, stripy zebras and beautiful birds. “I wish I could take photos of animals,” sighed Lisa.

“There are lots of interesting animals in the park,” said Grandma. “I’ll get my camera and we can take our own pictures.”
As they left the house, Lisa saw Grandma’s cat, Ginger, sleeping on the car roof. Click! She took her first photo.

In the park, Lisa saw a squirrel up a tree. Click! She took another photo. Lisa was so excited that she bumped into a little boy walking his dog. Lisa asked if she could take a picture and the boy said yes. Click! One perfect, puppy portrait.

Lisa watched a lady throwing scraps of bread on the path for some hungry birds. Click! Lisa took a picture of two funny seagulls fighting over a slice of bread. They made a lot of noise! "Silly seagulls," she giggled. "There's enough for everyone."

“I know a good place to look,” said Lisa’s grandma, pointing into the flower beds. Lisa kneeled down and peered through the leaves. She took pictures of a scuttling beetle, a squirming worm and a beautiful blue and purple butterfly.

When they got home, Lisa helped her grandma print out the photos and stick them in a scrapbook with glittery glue. "Maybe one day I'll take pictures in the jungle," said Lisa, "but right now, my park animal book is just perfect!"

Penny's Paddling Pool

It was a hot, sunny day and Penny and her dad were going swimming at the outdoor swimming pool. "I can't wait!" cried Penny. She ran up to the pool gates, clutching her armbands, then stopped in surprise. The pool was shut for repairs.

“Never mind,” said her dad. “We’ll go home and get out the paddling pool.” At home, Penny felt sad as she changed into her swimsuit. It wouldn’t be nearly as much fun splashing in a paddling pool as swimming in a real one.

Penny's dad turned the hose on and water splished and splashed into the pool. Penny got some of her special bubble bath from the bathroom and poured it in, filling the pool with frothy bubbles. Biscuits the dog was so excited, he raced round the garden.

Dad got an inflatable fish and frog for Penny to play with. Penny giggled as she floated the toys around and watched the bubbles drifting into the air. “Catch them, Biscuits!” cried Penny. “Woof, woof!” went Biscuits. He liked the bubbles, too!

“I’ve got a great idea,” said Penny’s dad. He disappeared into the garden shed and came out with the plastic slide. Dad hooked it over the side of the pool and Penny had her own water slide. “Whee!” she said, sliding down it. “This is brilliant!”

Whoosh! Penny whizzed down the slide again, making the toys bounce around in the bubbly water. “I thought the paddling pool wouldn’t be as much fun as the swimming pool,” she giggled, “but I was wrong. This is the best fun ever!”

Sarah's Sleepover

Sarah's friend, Marnie, had come for a sleepover. Even though they were best friends, Sarah and Marnie liked different things. "I want to be a princess," said Sarah, holding up a pretty dress. "I want to be a pirate, looking for treasure!" cried Marnie.

The girls wanted to go to the park in their outfits and Sarah's mum agreed. Marnie pretended she was the fierce captain of a pirate ship, searching for treasure. "Land ahoy!" she cried. Sarah pretended that she was a princess in the tallest tower of a beautiful, enchanted castle.

Sarah and Marnie were hungry after all their pretend play, so Mum took them home for a snack. “I’d like sticky, raspberry jam sandwiches, please,” said Sarah, with a smile.
“I’d prefer cheese, please,” said Marnie. “I don’t like jam.”
The friends ate their sandwiches. “Yummy,” they said, giggling.

Later on, when it was time for bed, Sarah put on her pyjamas and slippers, but Marnie put on a nightdress and bed socks. Then, Marnie chose a space story but Sarah wanted a story about a fairy ballerina. "I'll read both," said her mum, smiling.

When story time was over, the girls snuggled down. Mum tucked them up tight and kissed them goodnight. Marnie gave a big yawn and hugged her teddy. Sarah hugged her teddy, too. "I love my teddy because he's soft and cuddly," said Sarah.

"I love my teddy because he's soft and cuddly, too," said Marnie.
At last, the girls had found something they both liked.
"It doesn't matter if we like different things," said Sarah.
"We will always be best friends."

The New Bed

"Look, Mummy," said Rosie one morning, "my toes poke out at the end of the my bed!" Rosie loved her bed, but it was too small. "You've grown too big for it," said Mum. "I think it's time to get you a new one. Come on, let's go shopping."

Rosie and her mum went to the bed store. There were beds of all shapes and sizes. There were big ones, little ones and even two beds in one! Rosie didn't want bunk beds, though. "They're a bit plain," she said.

"This bed has got monsters on it," said Rosie. There were pink ones, green ones, spiky ones and hairy ones. Rosie and Mum looked at one another. "Too scary!" they cried together and burst out laughing.

Suddenly, Rosie ran to a bed with a play tent and slide.
"This is brilliant!" she cried, zooming down the slide. "I could play for ages on this, it's so much fun!"
"I think you would be too busy playing to get any sleep," said Mum, shaking her head.

Rosie wondered if she was ever going to find a bed. Then, suddenly, she saw something purple and soft and glittery and gorgeous. It was the most beautiful princess bed. “It’s perfect!” cried Rosie. “This is the bed I want.”

That night, Rosie settled down into her lovely new bed. Mummy read her a bedtime story all about a magical land. "Thank you, Mummy," said Rosie. "My new bed is perfect for me and I feel just like a proper princess!"

Silly Sports Day

Amy's cheeky cousins, Ella and Bella, had come to stay. "I hope they don't misbehave and mess up my room, like last time," whispered Amy. "They kept me awake all night, giggling."
"Don't worry," said Dad, "I've got a plan to keep them busy. We're having a princess sports day!"

Dad gave each girl a royal crown. Ella and Bella giggled as they put theirs on. “We’re going to win,” they said, teasing Amy. “Everyone go to the starting line for the obstacle race!” cried Dad. “Ready, set, GO!” They were off!

Ella and Bella raced ahead. They dived under tunnels, through hoops and around cones. Whoever found a pearl necklace and a wand won the race. Amy nearly took the lead, but Ella ran so fast, she crossed finish line first. "I won!" she cried.

Next was the three-legged race. Dad and Amy won by a mile because Ella and Bella kept falling over. No matter how many times they tried, they couldn't finish the race. They just ended up in a heap on the floor, breathless from giggling.

The egg and spoon race was lots of fun. The eggs wibbled and wobbled with each step. “Oh, no!” cried Amy, as her egg fell with a crack onto the ground. Ella lost her egg too, but Bella carefully crossed the finish line. “I won this time!” she cried.

“Well done, princesses,” said Amy’s dad. “You’ve all won a race. Now it’s time for a treat.” He brought out the picnic rug, a plate of sandwiches and some juice. “Here are your prizes,” he added, giving them each a delicious pink cupcake.

After the picnic, the girls played in the garden until it was time for bed. Amy was worried that Ella and Bella would mess up her room and keep her awake, but she was in for a surprise. When they went upstairs, the twins were really quiet.

Ella and Bella put on their pyjamas, brushed their teeth and got into bed. “Don’t you want to play or be silly?” asked Amy. “No,” replied Ella and Bella, “we’re too tired.” Amy smiled and snuggled down. Dad’s princess sports day had been a very good idea after all.

Julie's Dream

Julie loved dogs more than anything in the world. She loved big dogs, little dogs, hairy dogs and spotty dogs. She loved woofy dogs and yappy dogs. Julie loved dogs of every kind, but there was just one problem. She didn't have a dog of her own.

On the night before her birthday, Julie saw a shooting star whizzing past her window. "I'll make a wish to have my own puppy," said Julie, "but I don't really believe it will come true." Then, she climbed back into bed and snuggled down to sleep.

That night, Julie had a strange dream about a cute puppy. Julie played chase with him and they had fun for ages. He ran round and round, woofing and wagging his tail. He raced up to Julie and she was just about to scoop him up when suddenly, she woke up.

It was morning time. Julie jumped out of bed and ran downstairs.
"Happy birthday!" cried Mum and Dad.
"We've got some special presents for you," said Dad, "but first you need to open the back door. There is a surprise for you."
Julie was puzzled. What would the surprise be?

Julie soon found out. She opened the door and gasped to see the spotty puppy from her dream sitting there. This time, when she went to scoop him up, it was real. "My dream has come true," she said. At last, Julie had a gorgeous puppy of her own.